The Protector of Humanity
A Discourse of Value

Dr Julius Nang Kum

Ukiyoto Publishing

All global publishing rights are held by

Ukiyoto Publishing

Published in 2023

Content Copyright © Dr Julius Nang Kum

ISBN 9789360165901

All rights reserved.
No part of this publication may be reproduced, transmitted, or stored in a retrieval system, in any form by any means, electronic, mechanical, photocopying, recording or otherwise, without the prior permission of the publisher.

The moral rights of the author have been asserted.

This is a work of fiction. Names, characters, businesses, places, events, locales, and incidents are either the products of the author's imagination or used in a fictitious manner. Any resemblance to actual persons, living or dead, or actual events is purely coincidental.

This book is sold subject to the condition that it shall not by way of trade or otherwise, be lent, resold, hired out or otherwise circulated, without the publisher's prior consent, in any form of binding or cover other than that in which it is published.

www.ukiyoto.com

Late Pa Meh Lucas Tem

Preface

A good number of our children perform certain malicious acts not because they want to do so, but because they are ill-informed or uninformed. Apart from the knowledge they acquire in hard skills subjects such as Computer, Medicine, Physics, Mathematics, Biology, Geography, History, etc., many youths do not know that soft skills domains exist and these are the skills that also help in promoting success.

The purpose of this book is to initiate our youths into the world of values. Values are important because they build both hard and soft skills in humans which determine our success, but unfortunately, we constantly ignore them. Our brief investigation on values has revealed that many students do not know universal values, paramount values, academic values, national values, core values, and personal values. Based on these, this book is divided into four chapters.

Chapter One examines the most important universal value, which is the human life. It reveals who a true human being is and highlights instances to illustrate how human beings are stronger than other animals and how human beings are stronger than machines.

Chapter Two identifies the real nutrient of a human being, which is value. In this sense, the definition of value as used in the book is made, value hierarchy, value types, value sources and the characteristics of values are made known to our students.

Chapter Three offers only two important answers on why we need values. The first answer is to please our Creator and the second most important reason on why we need values in our lives is to succeed extremely well in our lives.

Chapter Four entertains our readers with some wisdom words drawn from diversified sources. These wisdom words form part of values which are aimed at feeding the human being in you.

It is not by mistake that Christ said "man shall not live by bread alone" (Jesus Christ; in Luke 4 verse 4), but also on other values such as love, respect, truth, justice, fear of the Lord, cleanliness, fine-tuned speeches, etc. Be a protector of humanity, and so a blessing to this world after having read this book.

Yaounde
Julius Nang Kum
August 2022

Contents

The Nature Of Human Being	1
Values	14
Why Do We Need Values?	43
Words Of Wisdom	51
About the Author	*62*

The Nature of Human Being

1.0 INTRODUCTION

In his effort to orientate humankind to changes, this intellectual writes: "What is necessary to change a person is to change his awareness of himself" (Abraham H. Maslaw; in Shepherd, 2016). This chapter identifies some qualities that are unique only to humans and not to Animals or machines. For the fact that only human beings possess these qualities, they give humankind an urge over other things such as animals, and machines plants. The aim here is to show the value of human beings which might have been neglected or not known by many persons especially our students, who are the future protectors or guiders of humans on earth. This ignorance or negligence on the values of a human being sometimes result to some people killing others, students shooting their friends or even their teachers, parents or teachers abusing their students and vice versa, husbands torturing or traumatizing their wives and vice versa. To illustrate the value of a human being, this chapter highlights how human beings are beyond the physical body, how human beings are beyond other animals, how human beings are beyond machines or robots. This is important because a sound knowledge of these characteristics might help us to know who we are and why we must love and protect our lives and the lives of other people irrespective of race, colour, faith, and gender.

1.1 BEYOND THE PHYSICAL BODY

Many students do not know who they are. For those students who do not know who they are, an answer to this confusion has been given by this great man: "*We are not human beings having a spiritual experience. We are spiritual beings having a human experience »*. (Teilhard de Charrdin; in shepherd,2016). Our success depends much on the above knowledge that we all are spiritual beings first, before putting on the human flesh. This implies a human being is made up of two entities:

the spiritual being and the physical being. The discussion below highlights some differences between the physical being and the spiritual being.

1.1.1 THE SPIRITUAL AND THE PHYSICAL EXPERIENCES

The discussion above has highlighted the notion of a human being as a spiritual being first before having a physical experience. We now turn to qualities of the physical being and those of the spiritual being that are found in a human being. In this light, read the quotation below.

What real basis is there for differentiating between human beings? Our bodies may be different in structure and colour, our faces may be dissimilar, but inside the skin we are very much alike, proud, ambitions, envious, violent, and sexual power- seeking. Remove the label and we are very naked; but we do not want to face our nakedness, and we insist on the label- which indicates how immature, how infantile we are (Krishnamurti)

In the citation above, Krishnamurti summarizes qualities that belong to the outer or physical human beings such as colour, different faces, and mentions those things that are common to the inner human being such as pride, ambition, and envy. He concludes by reminding us that we have remained so immature to identify these realities in us. However, the immediate two sections below detailly examine the outer human being and the spiritual human beings.

1.1.1.1 THE OUTER OR PHYSICAL HUMAN BEING

Some of the qualities of the outer human being have been highlighted above, such as colour, faces, and structure. The quotation below identifies in more details, aspects of the outer or physical human being:

"*The most common ego identifications have to do with possession, the work you do, social status and recognition, knowledge and education, physical appearance, special abilities, relationships, personal and family history, belief systems, and often political, nationalistic, racial, religious, and other collective identifications. None of these is you?* (Eckhart Tolle; in shepherd, 2016).

From the words of wisdom above, a sound matured mind will now argue that the qualities mentioned in the citation are found in people who think that they are human beings first and the spirit later. These persons who think that they are physical human beings first before the spiritual being spend all their time taking care or thinking about the colour of their skins, politics, greatness instead of taking care of their spiritual beings. In fact, this is not what a human being is. Your spirit comes first then the human experience follows. If this is maintained, then your success on earth must be natural and you will lead a life of a model and many generations must benefit from your lifestyle on earth. History has taught us that those who think and live with the notion that they are stronger than the spirit has failed countless times. In fact, those human being who begin by recognizing and honouring the spiritual human being first in them must succeed in their lives more than the persons who recognize the physical human being first. As a student who still has much to learn to transform this world to a better place, it would be better for you to feed your spiritual being well to tackle the physical being of yourself for your immense success in future. However, we do not glorify the inner being to the detriment of the outer being. We suggest that care should start from our inner being and flow to the outer being. That said, the discussion below examines some of the important needs of the outer being to protect or host the inner being.

- **Outer Human Being Needs**

A good knowledge of our inner – human being can be better understood if we know those basic things that the outer human being needs to stabilize the inner human being. This is important because a human being is a "spiritual being having a human experience"; Talking about the needs of the outer human being, Sheldon (2004) in Matsumato (2007: 1287) suggests that there are eight basic physical needs that are common in all human beings:

Eating

Drinking

Breathing

Sleeping

Eliminating

Having sex

Seeking shelter

Staying healthy

To attain these basic physical needs, Buss (1988,2001) in Matsumoto (Ibid:1287) highlights that there are some social problems that human beings must solved. These social problems include;

-Negotiating complex status hierarchies,

-Forming successful work and social groups

-Attracting mates,

-Fighting off potential rivals for food and sexual partners,

-Giving birth and raising children,

-Battling nature.

From the discussion above, we can now see that for us to be successful, we must satisfy the outer human being too and not only the inner human being. A good knowledge of what we have seen above will enable us to manage our relationships with another human being and nature. The discussion below examines our spiritual being and what it needs to be strong.

1.1.1.2 THE INNER OR SPIRITUAL BEING

The inner or spiritual human being is quite different from the outer or physical human being. Section 1.1.1 above has highlighted some qualities of the outer or physical human being such as colour. structure, and facial differences. This section now focuses on the inner or spiritual human being. The citation below tells us that:

Man is lost and is wandering in a jungle where real values have no meanings. Real values can have meaning to man only when he steps on to the spiritual path, a path where negative emotions have no use (Sai Basa; in shepherd, 2016)

The speaker above highlights the importance of stepping into the spiritual path. We learned that in the spiritual path, "negative emotions have no use". What are some of these negative emotions that can destroy or are useless to the spiritual human? The citation below identifies both negative and positive emotions:

As human beings we all want to be happy and free from misery --- we have learned that the key to happiness is inner peace. The greatest obstacles to inner peace are disturbing emotions such as anger, attachment, fear and suspicion, while love and compassion and a sense of universal responsibility are the sources of peace and happiness (Dalai Lama, in shepherd,2016)

Judging from the words of wisdom above, we can see that the inner or spiritual being of a human being comprises two qualities: those that can destroy and bring unhappiness, failure, misery, and those that can bring abundant happiness and success in our lives. In a way to emphasize on the negative qualities and some of their disadvantages, we read:

We plant seeds that will flower as results in our lives, so best to remove the weeds of anger, avarice, envy and doubt---"(Dorothy day; in shepherd (2016)

The speaker above calls those negative qualities "Weeds" which means they are unwanted plants on our farm. In fact, weeds are also plants like maize, and beans, but they destroy the real plants that we have planted and they need to be removed for our real plants to grow. As Dorothy Day calls them" Weeds", Dalai Lama names them "disturbing emotions". Everything being equal, our goal in this study is to examine those good qualities or "real plants" in our spiritual human beings that can enable us to succeed in all aspects in our lives irrespective of where we find ourselves. In this sense, we suggest you read these words of wisdom below.

"Love and kindness are never wasted. They always make a difference. They bless the one who receives them, and they bless you the giver (Barbara De Angelish) in shepherd 2016)

These things are known as values. these values enable us to interact with other people with little or no problems. As a student, so long as you embrace these values in your life then you can live and be successful anywhere. Some of these values that feed the spiritual side of the human being are honesty, love, kindness, and hard work, we will see them below.

THE POWER OF THE SPIRITUAL SIDE OF HUMAN BEINGS

As we have seen above, all human beings are first spiritual beings that put on the human flesh to experience everything that has to do with this world. The spirit is therefore using our bodies as its home, to experience the difficulties of this world. In this situation, the spiritual being is far stronger than the body and should be destroyed. Napoleon Bonaparte in his last days on earth, testified the fact that spirits are beyond destruction and will always triumph in any situation. This is what Napoleon Bonaparte said:

"Do you know what astonished me most in this world? The inability of force to create anything. In the long run, the sword is always beaten by spirit "(Napoleon Bonaparte; in shepherd 2016

In the citation above, Napoleon Bonaparte confirms the power of the spirit over anything such as force. If you can imagine an extra ordinary figure like Napoleon Bonaparte, who almost conquered the whole world, then we as learned citizens of this world should believe in what Napoleon Bonaparte says, that the spirits are stronger than anything on earth. The greatness of Napoleon Bonaparte is well known to mankind so much so that historians identified three things Napoleon Bonaparte did that changed the world. Talking about how Napoleon Bonaparte changed the world in three ways, Farah and Karl (198: T41) writes:

Although assessments of Napoleon differ widely, no one denies that he was one of the most colourful and famous people in all of history. He was also among the most influential. Napoleon helped spread the ideas of the French Revolution throughout Europe. The passages below discuss three additional ways Napoleon changed the world...

A-THE NAPOLEONIC CODE

"One of Napoleon's reforms ... was destined to have an impact far beyond the borders of France. That was the creation of the French civil code, the (Napoleonic Code). In many ways the code embodied the ideals of the French Revolution. For example, under the code there were no privileges of birth, and all men were equal under the law. At the same time, the code was sufficiently close to the older French laws and customs to be acceptable to the French Public and the legal profession. overall, the code was moderate, well organized, and written with commendable brevity and outstanding lucidity. As a result, the code has not only endured in France (the French civil code today is strikingly like the original (Napoleonic Code) but has been adopted, with local modifications, in many other countries".

B-THE INVASION OF SPAIN

"Napoleon also had a large, though indirect, effect on the history of Latin America. His invasion of Spain so weakened the Spanish government that for a period of several years it lost effective control of its colonies in Latin America. It was during this period of the de facto autonomy that the Latin American independence commenced".

C-THE LOUISIANA PURCHASE

"Of all Napoleon's actions ... the one that has perhaps had the most enduring and significant consequences was one that was almost irrelevant to his main plans. In 1803, Napoleon sold a vast tract of land to the United States. He realized that the French possessions in North America might be difficult to protect from British conquest, and besides he was short of cash. The Louisiana Purchase, perhaps the largest peaceful transfer of land in all of history, transformed the United States into a nation of near- continental size. It is difficult to say what the United States would have been like without the Louisiana Purchase; certainly, it would have been a vastly different country than it is today. Indeed, it is doubtful whether the united states whether the United States would have become a great power without the Louisiana purchase.

Napoleon, of course, was not solely responsible for the Louisiana Purchase. The American government clearly played a role as well. But the French offer was such a bargain that it seems likely that any American government would have accepted it, while the decision of the French government to sell the Louisiana territory came *about through the arbitrary judgment of a single individual, Napoleon Bonaparte*".

The citation above illustrates how powerful Napoleon Bonaparte was on this planet. Based on his greater experience of this world, then we should believe in what he says of the powerful nature of the spirit. If human beings are "spiritual beings having a human experience ", then we must endeavour to embrace those things that makes the spirit proud, such as love, kindness, and honesty.

2.2 BEYOND ANIMALS

For those people who are too exposed to the society, they might have heard other people compare human beings to animals in general and mammals. Many people have said that because human beings can feed their young ones or their babies with breast milk just as dogs or cows do to their puppies or to their calves respectively, human beings are like these mammals. Others have said that human beings have the same flesh with animals such as cows because when we eat excessive meat from the cows, our flesh develop gout to remind us or human beings that we have been eating another flesh that is like our own. In fact, there are many findings that have been done to remind us that humans are like certain animals like the apes. In fact, we have heard and read theories that remind us that humans developed from other animals like monkeys, gorillas, and chimpanzees. All the above findings and beliefs are sometimes genuine because we can prove them. Some hard-hearted individuals have used the above similarities to conclude that there are no great differences between a human being and some animals. This conclusion has made some people to beat others, to kill others, to steal from others, and to injure others. But as we have seen above, a human being is a spirit having a human experience. That alone is enough for us to know the value of a human being over other animals. Other big unique qualities that are observed only in human beings have been revealed by some researchers. Though many scholars have examined the qualities that are unique only to the humans, and which enable them to have a superior command over other animals, the discussion below focuses on the narration given by Matsumoto (2007:1291-1292) on the unique aspects seen only in the humans and not in other animals on earth.

2.2.1 LANGUAGE

Many findings have revealed that all animals on earth communicate among themselves in their different species. However, human beings are different from the rest of the animals because of their language. For example, human can create sounds to represent things, and emotions. Matsumoto (2007:1291) explains:

"All animals engage in environmental adaptation to survive; thus, all social animals may have culture, or at least a rudimentary form of culture consisting of social customs and adaptations (Boesch, 2003; Matsuzawa, 2001; McGrew, 2004; Whiten, Horner, & De Waal, 2005). Human cultures, however, are very different from animal's cultures, and these differences are rooted in several uniquely human cognitive abilities.

One is verbal language. Humans, unlike other animals, have the unique ability to symbolize their physical and metaphysical world (Premack, 2004), to create sounds representing those symbols (morphemes), to create rules connecting those symbols into meaningful words (lexicons), then phrases and sentences (syntax and grammar), and to put this all together in sentences (pragmatic). Moreover, since the use of papyrus in Greece and bamboo in china, humans have developed writing systems, so we can reduce those oral expressions to words on paper. This article is a uniquely human product.

From the explanation above, we can see how human beings are far developed in the ways they use and fashion language more than any other species of animals on the planet. In fact, just the fact that human beings can use a common language, no matter the race, no matter the nation, no matter the height, and no matter the religion makes them different from animals which do not have a common language amongst them.

2.2.2 INTENTIONAL AGENTS

Human beings can understand the intentions, the feelings, and the wishes of another fellow human being without any exchange of language. This makes them far superior to other animals, which cannot understand what another animal wants or wish without a sound. Matsumoto (ibid) explains:

Humans also uniquely can believe that other people are intentional agents. This ability begins at around 9 months of age (Tomasello, 1999). In one of Tomasello's most recent studies, for example, 18- month – old infants were presented with 10 different situations in which an adult experimenter had trouble achieving a goal (Warneken & Tomasello, 2006). One of these situations was when the experimenter accidentally dropped a marker and unsuccessfully tried to reach for it. More times than not, the infants were likely to help the adult experimenter, even though the experimenter never asked for help or made eye contact with the infant. The fact that human infants help others achieve their goals even though there is no direct benefit to the infant suggest that they understand other people's goals and an intrinsic motivation to help. These skills were not demonstrated in chimpanzees in the same study. Thus, we have causal beliefs, which form the basis for attributions, a uniquely human product.

From the explanation above, we are reminded how children remove our clothes or shoes from unwanted positions to the rightful places without us asking them to do it. Many animals cannot think of what might be good for another animal and they do it for them

2.2.3 SELF-OTHER KNOWLEDGE

Humans have certain values that govern themselves first before the society in which they live in. Some of these values are shame, disgrace, and guilt. Animals do not have these things. Matsumoto (ibid) explains:

Humans also have unique abilities concerning self-other knowledge. Clearly, other animals have knowledge or some conception of self. But humans are unique in that they have knowledge of self, knowledge of others, and knowledge that others know about the self (Tomasello, 1999). This knowledge is necessary to have morality, another uniquely human product. The existence of self – conscious emotions (Tangney & Fischer, 1995), such as shame, guilt, or pride, is also probably a product of this cognitive ability. The existence of this ability is probably why we do not just take off our clothes in the middle of the street, have sex any time we want to, or hit others whom we disagree with. Other animals, however, seem not to care as much.

From the quotation above, we observe that human beings too possess self- value and that of another fellow human being. This might explain why even mad persons cannot just stand in the middle of the street and pass out waste matter. In fact, they often look for a hidden place or in the night to do so. if not of this self-value our streets would have been littered with excrement from many mad men and women who parade our streets. If then a mad person knows the shame, that will hang on him or her by defecating publicly then there is that feeling of oneself and that of another person.

2.2.4 IMPROVE ON KNOWN KNOWLEDGE

One important unique quality of human beings is that they can improve on knowledge that is already known. In fact, cars that were made in the 1930s are not the same cars we find on our streets today. Animals find it hard to better their conditions in many domains. Matsumoto (ibid) explains:

Humans also have the unique ability to build continually upon improvements and discoveries. When humans create something that is useful, it is usually improved upon. This is true for computers, cars, audio music players, and, unfortunately, weapons of mass destruction and strategies for waging war. Tomasello, Kruger, and Ratner (1993) call this the ratchet effect. Like a ratchet, an improvement never goes backward; it only goes forward and continues to improve upon itself. The ratchet effect does not occur in other animals. Monkeys may use twigs to catch insects, but they never improve upon that tool. Humans not only make tools; they make tools to make tools, automate the process of making tools, and mass-distribute tools around the world for mass consumption.

From the speaker above we learn that human beings can constantly improve on known knowledge, known things, known relationships, known cities, known findings, known feelings, and known food.

If we can imagine these wonderful gifts from nature upon the human beings, it is worthy to treat our fellow human being with a lot of care irrespective of the person's age, colour, race religion, occupation, andnationality.

1.3 BEYOND MACHINES

In the proceeding section, the unique characteristics of human in relationship to animals have been examined. In our quest to highlight the fact that humans are beings of values, we now illustrate some unique qualities that are only in humans and not in machines and robots. In a finding on values, culture Action Europe 2018) states;

The skills needed to succeed in today's world and the future are curiosity, creativity, taking initiative, multi- disciplinary thinking and empathy. These skills, interestingly, are the skills specific to human beings that machines and robots cannot do--- The future of jobs and jobs training, PEW Research Centre, 2017

Some of the reasons we can put forward as to why only human beings possess some of the skills mentioned above come from the proceeding section. Because human beings are naturally endowed with skills such as language, a feeling for others, the ability to improve upon known knowledge, and with qualities such as curiosity, creativity, and taking initiative we can be easily developed more than machines. These specific qualities suggest that human beings are "Spiritual beings in human experiences". Nature seems to have prepared humans for the command of this world. However, many of us are ignorant of who we are. Research in many instances begins from our curiosity of whatever happens around us .From that vantage point of view, we can then raise many doubts and many questions .These are unique qualities found only in human and not in other animals or machines .The human mind is also capable of creating in the sense that, out of nothing ,the human being can solve a natural problem by inventing a machine or a tool that can assist him to solve that problem .In fact necessity is the mother of invention and so is the human mind. The idea of human being taking initiative has been highlighted in this study. Many calm and quiet minds have taken initiative to learn certain natural phenomena, to solve a problem, to help others, to pray for others, and even the initiative to die for others. The human mind is endowed with riches beyond our reach. Late professor Bate Bessong ones said that: *The human mind is like an ocean, All the rivers empty themselves into it, but the ocean never gets full.* The more the human mind accumulate knowledge, the more quest for more knowledge in even different fields. These are qualities that a machine or an animal cannot actually have. Empathy is just the ability to understand the feelings, the experience, the wants, the need, the wish etc. of another person without the person necessarily voicing it out to you. In fact, we have seen this above. Machine and animals cannot understand the feeling of another machine or animal and solve the problems without being told. With all these brief explanations, we think that human beings must be respected in every sense of world.

2.4 CONCLUSION

This chapter has identified some areas that make human beings important and vital for the transformation of this world. We have demonstrated cases to show that the physical human being is different from the spiritual human being, cases to show that human beings are above animals and cases to show that mankind is more than a machine or a robot. All these illustrations are aimed at reminding ourselves that no matter where a human being lives, works, no matter the colour, the age, the gender, the religion, the social status, the experience, the race, and the talent, we must take care of ourselves and other fellow human beings. In life, failure is certain for everyone. It is only when people start appreciating certain values in you that success start hovering over your head. Once you are conscious of values and respect those values that are highly appreciated in a culture, in a school, in a home, in a society, in a country, and in a person then people admit you in their midst and everything becomes manageable and you can succeed. Considering the importance of values in our lives and in our successful lives, the chapter below focuses on values.

Values

2.0 INTRODUCTION

The chapter above has demonstrated how, human beings are "spiritual beings having a human experience". The fact that all human beings are first spiritual beings before putting on the human flesh to feel human experiences demands us to examine some of the values that the spiritual being appreciate better. We have also mentioned that our success in life depends more on the state of our spiritual being. This means that once our spiritual being is low, which might be caused by vices such as shame, trauma, or any crime we might have committed, the physical body cannot function properly. The spiritual part of us is made up of good and bad values. We are interested in good values because they enable us to succeed in life. This chapter therefore focuses on the definition of values, their hierarchy and their types.

2.1 DEFINITION OF VALUES

The word value comes from a Latin word "Valerie" which means to be strong and vigorous". This might sound difficult to digest. However, Korhonen tells us the origin of value and those values that Aristotle identified thus:

According to Himmelfarb the concept "value" in its present sense comes from 1880s as Friedrich Nietzsche began to speak of "value" instead of "virtues", connoting the moral beliefs and attitudes of a society.

The quotation above reminds us that many centuries before the 1880s, the word value was not used. In fact, philosophers and other religious bodies were using the word virtue. In a way to illustrate this assertion, Korhonen (:138) explains:

Both in classical philosophy and religion, the concept used instead of value was a "virtue". For Aristotle the main virtues were wisdom, justice, temperance and courage, associated with prudence, magnanimity, liberality and gentleness. Then

Christian virtues faith, hope and love, as well as truth, righteousness and justice, were emphasized.

From the citation above, we observe that the concept of virtue was handled many centuries by philosophers such as Aristotle and he identified virtues such as wisdom, justice, temperance and courage. Since then, many findings have been carried out on virtues which we now call values.

In philosophy, the study of knowledge falls under epistemology, the study of reality under metaphysics, and the study of values is done under Axiology. (Tomar, 2014:51).

For those who might be interested in the various definitions of values, Mashlah (2015:158) summarizes:

If ten different people were asked to define "values" or what they understand by the term, we might have ten different definitions. Moore (1922) admits the difficulties of defining values – or its indefinability –because it is a simple quality like 'green'. Frondizi (1971) agrees with Moore (1922) regarding the difficulties of defining values; however, he disagrees with him as to why it is difficult to define. In contrast, Frondizi (1971) posits that the difficulties of defining values are due to their complexity, he considers values to have a Gestalt quality, which means that values do not just happen; instead, there is a need for them to be represented in some form of cognitive recognition, or via a transporter.

Based on the citation above, we can imagine how difficult it is to defines values. However, in his explanation of values, Thomas Hurka (? 1) says:

"The theory of value or of the good is one of the two main branches of ethical theory, alongside the theory of the right. Whereas the theory of the right specifies which actions are right and which are wrong, the theory of value says which states of affairs are intrinsically good and which intrinsically evil. The theory of the right may say that keeping promises is right and lying wrong; the theory of value can say that pleasure is good and pain evil, or that knowledge and virtue are good and vice evil. Since these states are not actions, they cannot be right or wrong, but they can have positive or negative value".

From the explanation above, a sound knowledge or awareness of values will enable you to know those qualities that are good for yourself, for your family, for the society in which you belong and those that are bad and may bring death, disgrace, and shame upon you and your society. However, our approach to values in this study hinges on the definitions given by Naagarazan (2006:2):

A value is defined as a principle that promotes well- being or prevent harm ", or values are our guidelines for our success our paradigm about what is acceptable.

values are those qualities that are acceptable by the society, by institutions, by organizations, and by individuals, which can enable you to live or be admitted as a member of a family, or society and be successful. As you can see, values are found in the inner or spiritual human being. To shed more light on the place and nature of values, these words of wisdom go thus:

"The best and most beautiful things in the world cannot be seen, nor touched ---but are felt in the heart" (Helen Keller; in shepherd, 2016). Besides the citation above, we can also read that:

"The more you recognize the immense good within you, the more you magnetize immense good around you" (Alan Cohen; in shepherd,2016)

In view of what we have seen so far, we can then conclude that a good knowledge of the values of a thing, a person, a family, an institution, an organization, a culture, and a nation will enable us to succeed in life. On the other hand, when we admit "Weeds" in our lives, they will open doors to curses, shootings, failures, fighting, frustrations, madness, imprisonment, and war. However, Schwartz &Bilsky (1987) in Mashlah (2015) identifies three worldwide human requirements' that form the foundation for all values:

- the necessity for biological survival,

- the request for social interaction,

-social and institutional demands for group wellbeing

Since our schools and the university and the higher education sector in general are contexts that generate knowledge, that rely heavily on human capital, that form leaders in the society, that protect every creation from non-living to the living, then human beings of high values are highly needed to manage all these situations.

2.3 Values Hierarchy

To shed more light on the hierarchical or the basic values that come first before the others, Naagarazan (2006:2) explains:

"Not all values have the same weight or priority. Some are more important than others and must be satisfied before others can be addressed. Dr. Abraham Maslow illustrated this with his hierarchy of human needs. Survival has a higher priority than security, which has a higher priority than social acceptance. Self-actualization can only be addressed to the degree that social acceptance is fulfilled. Similarly, self-actualization can only be pursued to the degree that self-esteem has been satisfied!

A keen look at the quotations above suggests that, your own life has the highest value before any other values. This is true because if you die now, your life will be taken away from this world. This means that secondary values such as honesty, humility, respect, neatness which you possessed will never be seen in you anymore. So human lives must be protected because that is the highest of all the values on the planet. Since human life has the highest value on this planet, it shall be of prime importance for us to understand chapter one above for the qualities of human beings. To shed more light on core values, Naagarazan (2016:3) then explains and classify core values into five groups. His discussion goes thus:

The five core human values are (1) Right conduct, (2) peace, (3) Truth, (4) love, and (5) Nonviolence.

1 Values related to RIGHT CONDUCT are:

A SELF – HELP SKILLS/ care of possessions, diet, hygiene, modesty, posture, self-reliance, and tidy appearance

B SOCIAL SKILLS: Good behaviour, good manners, good relationship, helpfulness, No wastage, and good environment, and

C ETHICAL SKILLS: Code of conduct, courage, dependability, duty, efficiency, ingenuity, initiative, perseverance, punctuality, resourcefulness, respect for all, and responsibility

Values related to PEACE are: Attention, calmness, concentration, contentment, dignity discipline, equality, equanimity, faithfulness, focus, gratitude, happiness, harmony, humility, inner silence, optimism, patience, reflection, satisfaction, self- acceptance, self- confidence, self- control, self-discipline, self-esteem, self- respect, sense control, tolerance, and understanding.

Values related to TRUTH *are: Accuracy, curiosity, discernment, fairness, fearlessness, honesty, integrity, (unity of thoughts, word and deed), intuition, justice, optimism, purity, quest for knowledge, reason, self-analysis, sincerity, spirit of enquiry, synthesis, truth, truthfulness, and determination.*

Values related to LOVE *are: Acceptance, affection, care, compassion, consideration, dedication, devotion, empathy, forbearance, forgiveness, friendship, generosity, gentleness, humanness, interdependence, kindness, patience, patriotism, reverence, sacrifice, selflessness, service, sharing, sympathy, thoughtfulness, tolerance and trust.*

Values related to NON- VIOLENCE *are:*

PSYCHOLOGICAL: *Benevolence, compassion, concern for others, consideration, forbearance, forgiveness, manners, happiness, loyalty, morality, and universal love*

SOCIAL: *Appreciation of other cultures and religions, brotherhood, care of environment, citizenship, equality, harmlessness, national awareness, perseverance, respect for property, and social justice.*

PERSEVERANCE *is defined as persistence, determination, resolution, tenacity, dedication, commitment, constancy, steadfastness, stamina, endurance and indefatigability. To persevere is described as to continue, carry on, stick at it (in formal), keep going, persist, plug away, (informal), remain, stand firm, stand fast, hold on and hang on. Perseverance builds character.*

ACCURACY *means freedom from mistake or error; conformity to truth or to a standard or model and exactness. Accuracy is defined as correctness, exactness, authenticity, truth, veracity, closeness to truth (true value) and carefulness. The value of accuracy embraces a large area and has many implications. Engineers are encouraged to demonstrate accuracy in their behaviour through the medium of praise and other incentive. Accuracy includes telling the truth, not exaggerating, and taking care over one's work.*

DISCERNMENT *means discrimination, perception, penetration, and insight. Discernment means the power to see what is not obvious to the average mind. It stresses accuracy, especially in reading character or motives. Discrimination stresses the power to distinguish or select what is true or genuinely excellent. Perception implies quick and often sympathetic discernment, as of shades of feelings.*

Penetration implies a searching mind that goes beyond what is obvious or superficial. Insight suggests depth of discernment.

The narration above has highlighted many human values that can guide you to success. A good mastery of these values is good both for you and the society. Because values are of many types and interwoven, the discussion below exposes you to many other values.

2.2 TYPES OF VALUES

One of the most important skill of a human being is the ability to classify things according to some similarities or differences. Many types of values exist in different classifications. Values are multi-functional in nature. For instance, the value honesty might be looked upon as a religious value, personal value, national value, and family value. In this section we present the classification of values according to major and individual classification. It should be noted that many works have been done on values and their kinds. In this study we narrow ourselves to general classification, Academic values, personal values and others.

2.2.1 Major Types of values

The discussion below is based on Lincoln - Douglas Debate paper. They suggest six most common major categories: They are major categories because you can fit some values into any of the six main types mentioned below.

Universal Values: These are values that there is nearly unanimous agreement as to the importance of them. These would include sanctity of human life, peace, and human dignity.

Instrumental Values: These are values that can be used to get something else. In other words, the value is an instrument which allows you to get some other things. Examples of these would include progress (which allows leisure time), Freedom (Through which we can get dignity and/ or self-actualization), and knowledge (which helps us get economic prosperity, and progress).

Intrinsic Values: Something has intrinsic worth simply because of what it is and not necessarily what it will lead to or because of its acceptance. Some possible examples of intrinsic values would include beauty, artistic expression, and happiness. We value them because they are an important aspect of life.

Prerequisite values: These are values that are necessary before you can get to some bigger goal. It is like the prerequisite course that you must take to get to the more advanced course. Some good examples of this type of value include safety (which is needed before people can even think about having anything else), Justice (which is needed before we can move onto equality), or the common good (which must be honoured if we can ever get to a state of peace).

Paramount values: Think of this type of value like you think of paramount studios with the large mountain. It is the value which is above all other things. Some examples of this might include freedom (which many people have given up their lives for and see as essential to a decent life) or sanctity of life (which if we do not value or have renders everything else worthless).

Operative values: This type of values are the ways that we make judgments on how to live the rest of our lives. We use these values as the overarching and guiding principles which tell us what is always right and wrong. These are things such as integrity, Honesty, and Loyalty

From the presentation above, we notice that many sub values can be fitted into any of the main categories. In your free period. You can pick up this challenge, look for more values and fit them into the main categories above.

2.2.2 Some Fundamental Values of Academic

In a work or a project entitled "The Fundamental values of Academic integrity", Keohane (1999: 11) says:

It can be difficult to translate values, even widely –shared values, into action-but action is badly needed now to promote academic integrity on our campuses. Researchers agree that rates of cheating among American high school and college students are high and increasing. Professor Donald McCase of Rutgers

University, founder of the centre for Academic Integrity, has found that more than 75% OF college students cheat at least once during their undergraduate careers. Particularly alarming is research gathered by Who is who Among High School Students indicating that 80 percent of high –achieving college –bound students have cheated, that they think cheating is commonplace, and that more than half do not consider cheating a serious transgression. New technologies have also made it easier to cheat. The Educational Testing service notes that one website providing free term papers to students has averaged 80,000 hits per day.

Drawing our inspiration from the citation above, we must highlight the fact that the phenomenon of cheating in our schools and universities is alarming. Besides the observation made above on cheating in schools and universities, we can also read this from Sherria L. Hoskins and Stephen E. Newstead (2009:27) thus:

A few years ago, a research team with whom one of us was working had a strong

suspicion that incidents of student cheating were related to their motivation for attending

university. The research team wanted to test this hypothesis but were faced with the

problem of how to measure student motivation. We were struck by how little research had

been done in this area, by how few measures of student motivation there were, and in

by how difficult it was to obtain a quick and readily usable indication of what

students' motives were for studying at university. This led us to consider how we could

identify, first, what motivates students, and, second, differences between types of

motivation.

As a member of an examination Brigade group created to check on any examination malpractices at the University of Yaoundé 1, we understand better the worries of keohane (1999) and Sherria L. Hoskins and Stephen E. Newstead (2009) on the growing phenomenon of cheating in our schools and universities. In fact, we have seen students swallowed papers which could be used as evidence to justify the fact that they were cheating in the examination room. Students have jumped over high walls to escape being caught during the examination period. These are ways to indicate that many students do not value their lives, do not value the examination, and do not value the knowledge they are supposed to acquire.

From the quotation above and from our own experiences, we can now see why our schools and our universities need good lessons on values because these institutions produce the finest of human beings for the society such as managers, leaders, priests, doctors, engineers, and pilots, who are supposed to guide, lead and protect the society. Talking about the key values that are needed in academics Fishman (2012:16) says:

The International Centre for Academic Integrity defines academic integrity as a commitment to five fundamental values: honesty, trust, fairness, respect, responsibility. We believe that these five values, plus the courage to act on them even in the face of adversity, are truly foundational to the academy. Without them, everything that we do in our capacities as teachers, learners, and researchers losses value and becomes suspect. When the fundamental values are embraced, utilized, and put into practice they become touchstones for scholarly communities of integrity. Rather than thinking of them merely as abstract principles, we advocate using the fundamental values to inform and improve ethical decision- making capacities and behaviour. The fundamental values enable academic communities to translate their ideals into action.

In a way to foster understanding, The Fundamental values of Academic Integrity explains the following values thus:

a)   Academic Integrity
Academic integrity is a way to change the world. Change the university first; then change the world (Young sup Kim ICAI Conference participant 2008)

b)   Honesty

Academic communities of integrity advance the quest for truth and knowledge through intellectual and personal honesty in learning, teaching, research and service.

c)   Trust

Academic communities of integrity both foster and rely upon climates of mutual trust. Climates of trust encourage and support the free exchange of ideas which in turn allows scholarly inquiry to reach its fullest potential.

d)   Fairness

Academic communities of integrity establish clear and transparent expectations standards, and practices to support fairness in the interactions of students, faculty, and administrators.

e)   Respect

Academic communities of integrity value the interactive, cooperative, participatory nature of learning. They honour, value, and consider diverse opinions and ideas.

f)   Responsibility

Academic communities of integrity rest upon foundations of personal accountability coupled with the willingness of individuals and groups to lead by example, upheld mutually agreed –upon standards, and act when they encounter wrong doing

g) Courage

To develop and sustaining communities of integrity, it takes more than simply believing in the fundamental values. Translating the values from talking points into action-standing up for them in the face of pressure and adversity requires determination, commitments, and courage.

From the findings of Fishman (2012:16), we observe that there are some key academic values, such as honesty, trust, and courage.

2.2.3 Some Core Values in Schools

In their investigation, Neasc (2016: 6) states some core values in schools:

Collaboration

Honesty

Perseverance

Respect

Personal integrity

Equity

Intellectual curiosity

Appreciation

2.2.4 Some Common Share Core Values

Besides our lives, some research bodies have observed that there are some values that are important on this world. Institute of Global Ethics, (2007:139) states:

We may ask, is there some basic for universal values that would be considered objective? The institute of Global Ethics states: "After more than a decade of doing research across the globe, we have discovered that while different people use different words to voice their values, the concepts nearly always can be distilled into a set of five or six shared values with a common subset: compassion, fairness, honesty, respect, and responsibility (We can see that some universal values are:

-Compassion

-Fairness

-Honesty

-Respect

-Responsibility

2.2.5 Plato Classification of values

Truth

Beauty

Goodness

2.2.6 Aristotle Classification of Values:

-wisdom

-justice

-temperance

-courage

2.2.7 Gandhi classification of Values
Truth

Non-violence

Freedom

Democracy

Equality

Self- realization

Purity of ends and means

Self-discipline

2.2.8 Spranger classification of values
Theoretical values

Economic values

Aesthetic values

Social values

Political values

Religious values

2.2.9 Parker classification of Values
Biological values

Economic values

Affective values

Social values
Intellectual values
Aesthetic values
Moral values
Religious values

2.2.10   Minutes Values

The list is not exhaustive, we only try to highlight some values that can guide people to success, by respect what individual, group, and society need. The list of values below is adapted from Gündüz (2016: 217).

National values

Patriot

National spirit

Country- nation

Tied to customs and traditions

Knowing where you come from

Tied to your history

National awareness

Nationalist

Knowing your past

Civilization

Protecting your culture

Knowing your ancestors

Respect for the police and the soldiers.

Knowledge –based values
Logical

Questioning

Creative

Educated

Successful

Knowing what you want

Curious

Open to changes

Investigative

Hardworking

Thinking analytically

Attention

Entrepreneur

Literate

Wisdom

knowledgeable

Enjoying learning

Thinking holistically

Having an aim

Having background

multilateral thinking

Authentic

Humanistic values
Endearment

Benevolent

Caring
Respect for human rights
Mature
Being a decent person
Not tolerating racism
Respect for feelings
Not discriminating
Not hurting even an ant
Being the real man
Accepting people as they are
Treating without judgment
Positive thinking
Eloquence
Loving people
Keeping your promise
Ability to communicate
Not classifying people
Naïve
Not eating your words
Telling people humanely the people
Respect for religious duties
Uncorrupted
Having your share of mankind

Communal values
Obeying the rules
Being useful for the society

Sharing
Manners
Being a leader
Political tolerance
Not harming others
Money
Respect for the elderly and the patients
Being respectable
Solidarity
Cooperation
Dignity
Be of good manners
Unity
Reconciled with society
Democratic
Respect for the disabled.

Universal values
Honesty
Love
Sacrifice
Kindness
Mercy
Trust
Virtue
Loyalty
Self-respect

Generosity
Helpfulness
Respect
Responsibility
Tolerance
Freedom
Fairness
Affection
Modest
Fidelity
Happiness

Leader's values
A] Personal values
Happiness
Health
Salvation
Family
Personal success
Recognition
Status
Material goods
Friendship
Success at work
Love

b Ethical –social values
Peace
Planet ecology
Social justice

c Ethical moral values
Honesty
Sincerity
Responsibility
Loyalty
Solidarity
Mutual confidence
Respect for human rights

d Values of competition
Money
Imagination
Logic
Beauty
Intelligence
Positive thinking
Flexibility

Religious values
Belief
Morality
Honour

Spirituality

Religionist

Chastity

Fairness

Strong-willed

Modesty

Learning Qur'an

Knowing the prophet

Being Grateful

Conscience

Wisdom

Love

Share

Faith

Cleanliness

Thankful

Inner Beauty

Humbleness

Virginity

Fear of God

Contented

Agreeing with one is right

Toleration

Decency

Obedient

2.2.11 PERSONAL VALUES

The list below gives you a wider range of some common values you might have been ignoring

Acceptance	Fast pace action	Power
Achievement	Financial rewards	Privacy
Adventure	Focus	Productivity
Altruism	Freedom	Promotion prospects
Ambition	Friendship	Reaching potential
Appreciation	Fun	Recognition
Authenticity	Happiness	Respect
Authority	Harmony	Responsibility
Autonomy	Health	Results
Balance	Helping others	Risk taking
Beauty	Honesty	Romance
Belonging	Humour	Routine
Challenge	Imagination	Security
Choice	Independence	Self-expression
Collaboration	Influence	Service
Commitment	Intellect	Sharing
Community	Intuition	Solitude
Compassion	Justice	Spirituality

Competition	Kindness	Status
Connection	Leadership	Success
Contribution	Learning	Teaching
Creativity	Love	Team work
Equality	Loyalty	Tolerance
Excellence	Making a difference	Tradition
Excitement	Nature	Travel
Expertise	Nurturing	Trust
Fairness	Order	Variety
Faith	Passion	Winning
Fame	Peace	Wisdom
Family	Personal growth	Zest for life

Source: Circle of Life, 5276 Hollister Ave Ste 257, Santa Barbara, CA 93111 805-617-3390 *http://www.circleoflife.net*

2.3 CHARACTERISTICS OF VALUES

There are many characteristics of values, which are identified below. However, the most important one is that value constantly change. For example, the value of a bunch of plantain can change from 1000 FRS to 500 FRS depending on the season, the quantity in the market, the relationship between the seller and the buyer, and the source of the plantain. For instance, if the bunch of plantain is stolen, the thief can sell it for even 250 FRS to escape. Same goes to personal values. The society might look upon you as a person of high moral or social values, but if you are caught cheating, fornicating, stealing, corrupting or telling lies, the high value they had for you might falls to a level unbelievable. In fact, many persons of high values in our society always try as much as possible to protect their dignity from being destroyed. Talking about some characteristics of values, Frey (1994: 19-24) explains:

1.   All values are learned values. Not unlike the acquisition of a language, values are transmitted and inculcated through an intricate web of societal agents and interactions. Primary to this web are family members and social peers, formal schooling, leisure, work and religious activities, and such rites of passage as baptism, confirmation and marriage. And interwoven throughout this web is the oral and /or written word, the stories of a people. The influence of this web is particularly important during childhood when the basic value parameters are established. In turn, these parameters help orient the subsequent acquisition and the reaffirmation of values throughout a person's life span.

Because values are learned, they can be forgotten, and they can be learned anew, though usually only with great effort. But values can be changed. Humanity is neither innately predisposed to certain values; nor is the content of values genetically determined. My concern here is not to suggest how an individual form his or her values. Furthermore, these comments are not meant to preclude the insights of such theorists as Noam Chomsky, Erik Erikson or Jean Piaget. The possibility that humans have certain biologically – based maturation levels and predispositions influencing the acquisition of language and personality must be considered in any discussion of the acquisition of values. Suffice it to say, the formation of an individual's value configuration is an extremely complex process.

2.   Values are relatively enduring. Values are grounded in the cultural heritage of a society and pervasively housed within the institutions of the society, the web. And values are well established from childhood. An individual may decide to forego a value, only to be confronted by it at each juncture within the web of society and to be grounded by its parameters formed early in life. The values of a society or of an individual are not easily altered.

3.   Values are not necessarily consciously known by either the individual or society. Not unlike our everyday linguistic grammar, values are seldom overtly articulated, even though we depend upon both in comprehending another's action and in generating our own. Your search for your own values and the values of others is accomplished only with great effort.

4   Values tend toward consistency, i.e., like values. The assemblage of an individual's or of a community's values strives for affiliation, compatibility and integration among those values. If a value is not consistent with the assemblage of values already held, it is not easily integrated and is often ignored and excluded.

This is not to suggest that we will always find consistency among the values held by any given individual or expressed in each community. Values strive for consistency. The assemblage of values of an individual or community is typically inclusive of disparate and often mutually contradictory values. It may even be the case that a configuration of values not only accommodates but espouses seemingly contradictory values. At issue is not the inconsistent disposition of an individual values in question, but the overall structure of the relationships and the character of that integration among all those values. To understand any given value, one must also consider the larger gestalt in which it is embedded. Such a contradiction will be observed when we discuss the Crow Indian values of oneness and unity, differentiation and uniqueness. The apparent inconsistency is dissolved when the specific contextual integration, in this instance, the imagery of the "circle" and "wagon wheel,» is taken into consideration.

5.   Values enshrine and impact a society's concepts of the *morally desirable*. Values set forth the social criteria for and the cultural assumptions upon which good and bad, right and wrong, moral and immoral, noble and vile are established. Values provide a code and form the basis for all moral judgments, whether directed at others, nature or the self. Values guide human conduct, providing a "road map" for action. Of course, what one may value as proper, another may value as immoral and improper. Therefore, values are often at the focal point of conflict.

6.   Values are inundated with *feelings* and are held with strong conviction. There can be no passively neutral values. Fear, sympathy, hate, love, anger, passion, contempt: all are expressions of this subjective dimension of values. Values are most assuredly felt.

Because of this affective component, values are thus more than a code of conduct. By infusing judgments with passion, values establish the desirable. Good and bad are not simply laid out; "good" is passionately desired and "bad" is ardently avoided. Values are the great *motivators* within a society and the individual; the drive directed towards all sorts of ends. From how a "rich man" is defined to what is most "feared" in life: all are grounded in values. But it is also this passion that certainly can inhibit an appreciation of values different from one's own. Emotions can cloud a clear vision.

7.   Values establish a *disposition* to act. Values influence our behaviours by preparing us to act in certain morally- oriented ways. When a certain behavioural response is called for in each context of social interaction, what that behaviour may be is based in part upon the values held. I suggest "in part" because values, while primary among those influences, are not the sole influence on our behaviours. Other influences include the level of individual self- esteem, social role definitions, societal laws, spontaneous collective behaviour and the persuasiveness others, for instance. Consequently, identified values alone are not necessarily accurate predictors of behaviour. While they closely parallel one another, the values we hold and the behaviours we exhibit are not the reverse sides of the same coin, each synonymous with the other.

8   Any given value is based upon and expressed in terms of certain *epistemological criteria*. Upon what standard of knowing is a value acknowledged and represented? How is a value validated by the holder of that value? In what terms is a value framed and publicly presented? To assert, for example, that "wilderness is a vast, yet untapped natural resource to be harvested" implies a value based upon and expressed in terms of "commodity" that has "production value," and that can be distributed and consumed.

2.4 SOURCES OF VALUES

Under normal conditions, values should be acquired wherever one finds oneself. Values should be learned at home, in family meetings, on farms, in gardens, in schools, at the university, in churches, in offices, in the market, in shops, and garages. These are some common sources of values from an unknown source:

1. Life Experience:

Many values originate out of the experiences of the individual and those of his fellow men. Men constantly keep on determining what values they must follow to find happiness and fulfil their destiny as human beings. These source orientations are conformed by Radhakrishnan (1950) who observed, «Values in education although they find their source in philosophy, have a second source in society, the people, their culture and their ideals".

2. Cultural background:

Our values are usually grounded in the core values of our culture, which reflect culture's orientation to five basic problems viz.,

- ❖ Beliefs of child rearing and social control
- ❖ The attitude to take nature as fatalistic or seeing it as a challenge to be conquered in the interest of man's comfort
- ❖ The question whether man should live for the present or future.
- ❖ The kind of activity most valued; and the kind of inter-personal relationship whether it is competitive or cooperative

3. Religious background

In its pursuit of truth religion is also concerned with values. Many basic values are Common to all religion.

4. Scientific background:

It helps us to make value judgments only to the extent that we relate it to value assumptions. New information on scientific front need not pose a threat even if it requires a change in the present frame of reference.

No matter the source, it is our undying wish that wherever one finds oneself, the urge to learn Values should be developed. Those who are fishing, hunting, building, and tapping, should preach the gospel of values to their mates, friends, children and wives.

5. Sources from Mashlah (2015:162)

Culture

Religion

Economy

Society

Politics

Family

Philosophy

2.5 THE IMPORTANCE OF VALUE EDUCATION

Many scholars have advocated for the need for value education in our society. One of these scholars is Tomar. In his work, Tomar (2014: 52) writes:

Value based education is a tool which not only provides us a profession but also a purpose in life. The purpose of our life is undoubtedly to know oneself and be ourselves. Value based education is a key dimension of building peace, tolerance, social conduct, justice and intercultural understanding. For the real progress of a country, it is very necessary to develop values in all citizens and to achieve this goal, teachers plays an important part. Teachers are key for knowing or understanding a nation, in the other words they are the builders of a nation. So, to make the significant development in a nation or society we must look towards teachers. This we can hope to achieve sound development of personality of a teacher has a positive effect." A teacher can play an important role in promoting this discussion because a teacher has the capacity to influence students with their thoughts, and personality and engage them in these activities. The teacher must *never impose ethical codes or standards of behaviour: these should arise out from social situation and the pupil's evaluating of his own behaviour. Raise a child to understand how to relate well with other people and righteousness opens doors to many opportunities*

From the quotation above, we learn that "righteousness opens doors to many opportunities ". Therefore, value education should open many doors to our talented children.

Experience has shown that honest students even though they might be dull have succeeded in life more than highly talented but dishonest, proud students. Many of the causes of value degeneration in our society can be read from Tomar (2014 :52) thus:

The main problem of present time is 'deterioration of values in human beings. Corruption is increasing day by day. Material advancement made us greedy and selfish. Nobody is careful about maintaining the values. When we go through newspapers, T.V and other agencies, we come to know about many crime activities, which are very much shocking for the human beings. Therefore, the modern poet T. S. Eliot has called this world 'A Waste Land' where men are spiritually dead amid unappalled material progress and miraculous scientific achievement. There are so many challenges, but some of these are mentioned here:

-Nuclear family system decreases the values because parents have not much time for their children. In joint family a great ideal of care, love and wellbeing. The old received as much care and attention as the very young and the all children were shared by a sort of common wealth and a source of joy and happiness. Story telling have always been an effective way of presenting values, concepts and ideas.

-Misdirected education system instead of developing a person as human being it is only directed towards superficial, surface level achievement. Education is nothing today but a profit-making business, it will go on to become our source of bread and butter. It is designed purely for money making and not for man making and only promotes negatives qualities like jealousy, hatred and rivalry instead of virtues like kindness, compassion and honesty.

-Shortage of well –trained dedicated teachers, value-based curriculum, innovative teaching methods, materials and service learning approach.

-Today there is a rapid advancement in technology and science taking place. With the rise in material advancement, we are lacking our cultural and moral standards. There is more greed, more selfishness, lack of sincerity and integrity.

-Politics oriented student's unions.

-Media is one of the leading causes for value deterioration. Television videogames, music lyrics that have violent connotations has a negative effect on child' psychology.

-Tit for that attitude, demanding nature of children, self-interest dominates public interest, no interest in religious practices, no respect for elders and teachers.

-Lack of refresher programs, scholarships for teachers, extra burden of work like election, polio drops, guiding duty, census survey etc. and absence of sacrifice among teachers for their students.

-Urbanization has bad impact on the culture and rural life values, including socialization.

-The causes of value degradation in our society has been highlighted by the above writer. In fact, there are many causes in different situations and even different locations. The quotation above only serves as a trigger to let us know that some activities in which we involve ourselves can be very destructive to our children and even us. So, we need a strong based value up- bringing to be successful in many domains, after all, righteousness open doors to many opportunities". So, we must avoid contact with sources of degrading values.

The scholar in the citation above has enumerated some of the causes of degrading values in our society. The causes are not exhaustive. You can look for more causes and add, based on your culture, your experience, and your religion.

2.6 CONCLUSION

Having identified the spiritual being and the strength this spiritual being has over the body; this chapter was aimed at highlighting those things that the spiritual being needs to function well. In this sense, this chapter has examined the definition of values, the importance of valued education, sources of values, the need of valued education and some characteristics of values. As already mentioned so far, values are many and they change based on places, individuals, time, taste, fashion, families. Countries, and cultures. It is your duty to know the values that your school, your family, your father, your mother, and your teacher and your friend. By knowing the values of each of these individuals or places, you can then respect them to live a happy and prosperous life.

Why Do We Need Values?

3.0 Introduction

The first chapter above has reminded us that the most important value we have is our own lives. This is so because if we are dead, people will not be able to see other values in us such as love, cleanliness, honesty, respect, fear of the lord, and intelligence. Thus, we must protect ourselves, protect other people, protect our animals, protect our studies, and protect our relationships. In this chapter, we will examine why we need values to succeed first in the spirit being and in the human being, because Jesus Christ in Matthew 6 verse 33 said "But seek first his kingdom and his righteousness, and all these things will be given to you as well". In other words, keep your spirit clean first and your body will automatically become clean because "we are spiritual beings having a human experience". Look at these words of wisdom again: *"We are not human beings having a spiritual experience. We are spiritual beings having a human experience »*. (Teilhard de Charrdin; in shepherd,2016). Therefore, this chapter talks about the importance of values according to prophets and values according to intellectuals

3.1 To Make our Creator Happy

Remember you are becoming an important member of your family, an important member of your compound, an important member of your quarter, an important member of your village, an important member of your town, your city, your country, your continent and the world in general. As a human being of this century, you do not need to be a Christian, a Muslim, a Hindu, a Buddhist, a Babi, a Baha'i, a Judaism or a Zoroastrian to know that our creator demands good values from you. Our parents might have done so out of ignorance because many could neither read nor write. Our case is quite different because we can read and write. The only problems we might have now can be laziness and stubbornness, which are bad values for a dynamic generation like ours. As a future intellectual you must know that the knowledge we get from books or from important leaders is known as authoritative knowledge. Authoritative knowledge is the most respected source of knowledge because it is based on facts or important findings or research which can be further verified. That said, you must know that some intellectuals have kept records on those exceptional human beings who in one moment or the other talked about our heavenly father. These men of God, or prophets preached about values and nothing else. Even the son of God while on earth preached only of LOVE which is the most important value. The analysis below might broaden your mind on some of these important prophets and even the son of God and what they preached.

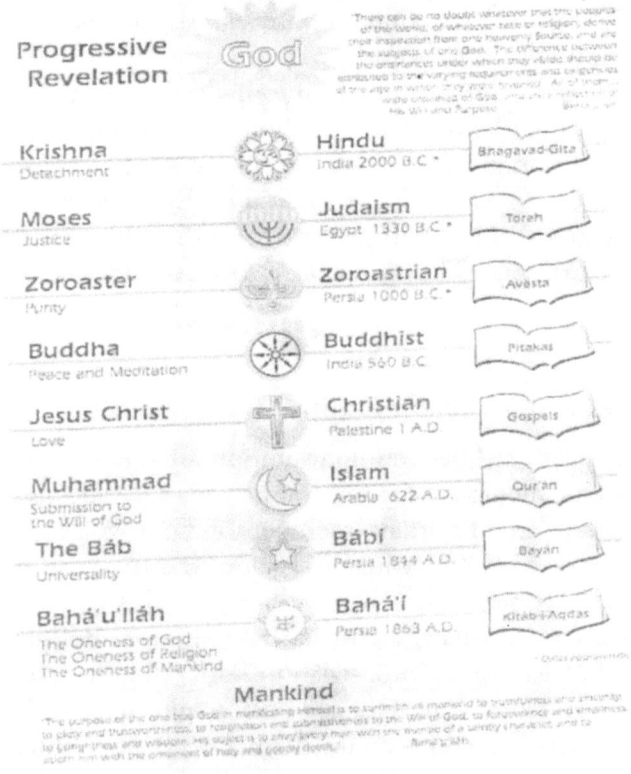

The analysis above is known as Progressive Revelation. It broadens our knowledge on those important prophets who preached about God. From the document, we will describe only three figures: Moses, Jesus Christ and Muhammad because they are popular to us. Talking about Moses, we can observe that he was born in Egypt around 1330 BC, his religion is known as Judaism, his books are known as the Torah (Genesis, Exodus, Leviticus, Numbers, Deuteronomy) the value he preached was JUSTICE. Jesus Christ was born in Palestine in the year 1 AD, his religion is known as Christianity, his books are known as the Gospels, and the value he preached was LOVE. Muhammad was born in Arabia around 622 AD, his religion is Islam, his book is Quran, and the value he preached was SUBMISSION TO THE WILL OF GOD.

Amongst the three figures described above, (Moses, Jesus Christ and Muhammad) we can further focus on Jesus Christ because of his exceptional nature, the availability of convincing documents about him, and the miracles he performed. All these were for the sake of LOVE. Jesus Christ, preached, practiced, embraced, and died for the sake of "LOVE".

To know how, what, where, when and to whom Jesus Christ preached, practiced, embrace and died for LOVE from when he was born, you read his Gospels according to Matthew, Mark, Luke and John in the Holy Bible. But if you wish to understand how Jesus Christ stood for LOVE from the womb to the tomb, let us understand the atmosphere in Judea before he was born and into which he was born. That said, it should be known that Christ was born in a troublesome period between the Romans army and the Jews in Judea. The detailed story is narrated in Mc Kay et al (1983:184), thus:

In A.D 40 the emperor Caligula undid part of Augustus' good work by ordering his statue erected in the temple at Jerusalem. The order, though never carried out, further intensified Jewish resentment. Thus, the Jews became embittered by Roman rule because of taxes, sometimes unduly harsh enforcement of the law, and a misguided interference in their religion.

Among the Jews two movements spread. First was the rise of the zealot's extremists who worked and fought to rid Judaea of the Romans. Resolute in their worship of Yahweh, they refused to pay any but the tax levied by the Jewish temple. Their battles with the Romans legionaries were marked by savagery on both sides. As usual, the innocent caught in the middle suffered grievously. As Roman policy grew tougher, even moderate Jews began to hate the conquerors. Judaea came increasingly to resemble a tinderbox, ready to burst into flames at a single spark.

The second movement was the growth of militant apocalyptic sentiment- the belief that the coming of the messiah was near. This belief was an old one among the Jews. But by the first century A.D. it had become more widespread and fervent than ever before. Typical was the Apocalypse of Baruch, which foretold the destruction of the Roman Empire. First would come a period of great tribulation, misery, and injustice. At the worst of the suffering, the Messiah would appear. The messiah would destroy the Roman legions and all the kingdoms that had ruled Israel. Then the messiah would inaugurate a period of happiness and plenty.

This was no abstract notion among the Jews. As the ravages of war became ever more widespread and conditions worsened, increased people prophesied the imminent coming of the messiah. One such was John the Baptist, 'the voice of one crying in the wilderness', "prepare ye the way of the Lord". Many Jews did just that. The sect described in the Dead Sea scrolls readied itself for the end of the world. Its members were probably Essenes, and their social organization closely resembled that of the early Christians. Members of this group shared their possessions, precisely as John the Baptist urged people to do. Yet this sect, unlike the Christians, also made military preparations for the day of the messiah.

Into this climate of Roman severity, fanatical zealotry, and messianic hope came Jesus of Nazareth (Ca 3 B.C –A 29). He was raised in Galilee, the stronghold of the zealots. Yet Jesus himself was a man of peace. Jesus urged his listeners to love God as their father and each other as God's children. The kingdom that he proclaimed was no earthly one, but one of eternal happiness in a life after death.

From the narration above, we learn that Jesus came into this world in a moment that there was tension between the Romans colonizers and the Jews, or his country people in Judea. The Romans were taxing his people, the Romans army was torturing or even killing his people because Jesus' people or the Jews especially in Judea where Jesus was born were constantly rebelling against the Roman occupation, and Roman laws. But under this suffering, Jesus' people or the Jews kept on crying and praying that God will one day send them a saviour sooner than later, a Messiah who will destroy the powerful Roman army and occupation over them.

In fact, in all these sufferings, in all these taxes, in all these tortures and killings, in all these impositions by the Romans, in all these weeping and mourning, in all these cries to God to send a saviour to save them from the hands of the Romans, Jesus was present. He saw the beatings of his people, he saw the killings in his country, he saw his country people crying day and night in temples praying for a saviour from God. Jesus knew that he was that True Messiah, that True Saviour that his people were praying for to free them from the beatings, from the tortures, from the imprisonment, and from the killings.

Besides all these odds in his presence, Jesus had all the potentials we can imagine to stop all those troubles. what a man? If Jesus was a proud and a tribalistic human being like you and I, he would have turned and asked God to send ten million or more angels to destroyed the Roman army into ashes in Judea first, then to the Roman capital where the Roman Emperor on the throne would had been killed and reduced into ashes in a twinkle of an eye. If the anger continued in him as it would had done in you and I, Jesus would had raided and destroyed the rest of the world to show to his country people that he was that true messiah they had been waiting for years. On the contrary we have seen Jesus who despite all these horrible treatments to his people, and the unthinkable power he had to stop them, did nothing horrible. He did not kill a Roman child, he did not kill a Roman woman, he did not kill a Roman soldier like you and I would had done. Jesus instead said give to Caesar what belongs to Caesar. If you were a Jew in that period, you would had doubted and even asked Jesus to stop those noises of his, that he was the Messiah, that he is the King of the Jews, that he is the Saviour of the Jews, that he is the child of God, and was still that he was the owner of heaven and earth. However, this is what happened and it is our function to think over this situation and admire Christ the more. All these to protect love for all mankind. From this case above, Christ teaches us many moral lessons such as:

-do not miss your focus because of situations *(*for example, Jesus' mission on earth was to serve all mankind and not only his country people)

-do not reveal your identity *(*for example, Jesus was that messiah but he remained silence until people started discovering who he was)

- **do not misuse any power at your command** (for example, Jesus could destroy the Romans in a second but he did not do so)

-do not discriminate on the bases of nationality, colour, tribe. Social class, age, and gender. (for example, Jesus did not kill the Romans because they were from a different nation or tribe)

-do not allow anger override you *(*for example, Jesus was not carried away by anger in that atmosphere of problems, instead he preached love one another)

-**understand the works of God** (for example, why did God send Jesus into this world only in that period of tension and in that place? because God wanted us to see how a good person like his son can go through a horrible situation and still preach love for one another without fear)

From the illustration above, we can observe how God's servants preach values and they are ready to die for them as Jesus Christ did. You Creator demands good values from you to be happy, so do not disappoint him.

3.2 To Succeed on Earth

As soon as you do not disappoint God, then the respect and protection of good values will make you to succeed on earth, no matter your family, your village, your town, your country, your continent, your colour, your religion, your social class, your gender, your age, your health, your level of learning, your finances, and your effort. How is this possible? This is possible because a human being has two skills: the hard and the soft skills. Talking about the differences between the hard and the soft skills, Sandi Melkonian explains:

Hard skills are easily recognizable as those required for success in a discipline. Among some of these are calculus, statistics, chemistry, finance, accounting, anatomy. Intuitively we understand the need for these static skills in their professional realms. They are unchanging from job to job, company to company, or even boss to boss unless it involves something unethical. Hard skills engage left-brain thinking. Soft skills on the other hand are less easily defined, highly dynamic, and utilize right brain thinking. Investopedia defines them this way, "Soft skills have more to do with who we are than what we know. As such, soft skills encompass the character traits that decide how well one interacts with others, and are usually a definite part of one's personality. Whereas hard skills can be learned and perfected over time, soft skills are more difficult to acquire and change."

In the discussion below, we will highlight the nature of these skills and remind you that these skills depend on good values.

3.2.1 Hard Skills

As you must have read above, hard skills reveal "What You Know'. In describing hard skills, Wibowo et al (2020 :557) explain:

According to Bahrumsyah (2010) hard skills are the mastery of science, technology and technical skills related to their field of knowledge. According to Syawal (2010) hard skills are more oriented towards developing the intelligence quotient (IQ). From these two opinions, it can be concluded that hard skills are the ability to master technological knowledge and technical skills in developing intelligence quotient related to their fields.

From the explanation above, we observe that hard skills stand for what you know. In other words, can you type, can you do research, can you analyse, can you write, can you drive, can you build a house, can you electrify a home, can you teach, can you fly an aeroplane, can you do engineering, and can you weave?. In fact, you cannot succeed in knowing anything if you do not respect your Creator, your father, your mother, your teacher, and your mates. Accordingly, without good values, we cannot acquire hard skills easily.

3.2.2 Soft Skills

Unlike hard skills that stand for "what you know", soft skills reveal "who you are". Talking about soft skills, Wibowo et al (2020:556) summarize:

Thus, it can be concluded that the definition of soft skills is a person's ability to relate to other people (interpersonal skills) and a person's ability to regulate himself (intrapersonal skills) as well as a person's additional ability to trust / care for both the creator and other people (extra personal skills).

From the explanation above, we can notice that soft skills are important for our success in life, because we must be able to interact with ourselves, interact with others and interact with our creator. All these interactions demand a good mastery of good values.

3.3 Conclusion

This chapter has identified some of the advantages of knowing some of the basic values highlighted in chapters one and two. We have learned that a good knowledge of good values and a good maintenance of them can enable us to be closed with God. It has been demonstrated beyond doubt that all the servants of God to this world preached and died because of values. We also observed that a sound knowledge of values can also enable us to be successful in anything we embark on. To justify this, the chapter identified two important skills needed by every human being for a successful end. At this moment, we hope that you have learn anything that can push you to learn more or to embrace some of the values you had ignored.

Words of Wisdom

4. Introduction

Secondary education that comprises the secondary and high school sections is the most exciting section of the educational system after the ignorant primary section and the future mature tertiary section. This is so because many, if not all students arrive their puberty stage at the secondary level. The age of puberty is characterized by unnecessary excitement, boldness, cleanliness, beauty, handsomeness, sexual urge, a lot of comparison, worries, anger, and hastiness. Any normal person will acknowledge the fact that all these things cited above can easily mislead a child into unwanted pregnancy, drug abuse, dishonesty, and stealing. Since the secondary section of education includes the high schools, much knowledge is acquired during this period and as Dalai Lama once said "The period of greatest gain in knowledge and experience is the most difficult period in one's life" (Dalai Lama; in Shepherd, 2016). From these wise words, we need to help our students and we also pray that our students too must overcome this period with self-courage. Self-courage because you can take a horse to the stream but it refuses to drink. This means that no matter the assistance your parents, your teachers or friends can give to you, if you are not willing to change, nothing can be done to better your condition. In a more serious voice, for us to fight against these vices, children need the help of religious leaders, wise men, experienced teachers, good friends and caring parents. This chapter focuses on some common wise words which we think can inspire some students.

1.2 WORDS OF WISDOM

Below are a good number of words of wisdom. These words come from people who have experienced certain phenomena, certain things, certain people, and certain obstacles for long and think that their experiences can also help other fellow human beings in one aspect or the other to succeed. Success in most cases goes to those individuals who listen to wise people, who read wise books, who attend educative meetings, who live with wise people and in wise societies. Success hates noise and publicity especially when success is still young. The words of wisdom below are gathered from many sources: Shepherd (2016), BBC, the Holy Bible, Zhoa village, Chinese and African Proverbs. These words of wisdom are not classified as in shepherd (2016). They are given in a mixed form and demands you the reader to cling to anyone that might help you in one way or the other. It would be better to read these words of wisdom to the point that you chew and digest them as Francis Bacon once said about reading "Some books are to be tasted, others to be swallowed and some few to be chewed and digested".

4.2.1 If someone curses their father or mother their lamp will be extinguished (Proverb 20:20).

4.2.2 A cock belongs to the owner, but when it crows, it crows for the whole village'. (Zhoa- African proverb) (It says you are a citizen of a nation. But when you become popular, that success or popularity belongs to the whole planet).

4.2.3 It is your decision not your conditions that truly shape the quality of your life "(Anthony Robbins)

4.2.4 One important key to success is self –confidence. An important key to self – confidence is preparation (Arthur Ashe).

4.2.5 Only in quiet waters things mirror themselves undistorted. Only in a quiet mind is adequate perception of the world. (Hans Margolius)

4.2.6 Associate yourself with men of good quality if you esteem your reputation, for t'is better to be alone than in bad company (George Washington)

4.2.7 Destiny is not a matter of chance, it is a matter of choice, it is not a thing to be waited for, it is a thing to be achieved (Jeremy Kitson)

4.2.8 Wise men speak because they have something to say; fools because they have to say something (Plato)

4.2.9 If people know how hard I had work to gain my mastery; it wouldn't seem wonderful at all" (Michelangelo)

4.2.10 If you think you are too small to be effective, you have never been in the dark with a mosquito (Betty Reese)

4.2.11 When you make people angry, they act in accordance with their baser instincts, often violently and irrationally. When you inspire people, they act in accordance with their higher instincts sensibly and rationally. Also, anger is transient whereas inspiration sometimes has a life – long effect" (Peace pilgrim)

4.2.12 We cannot build the future for our youths, but we can build our youths for the future (Franklin D. Roosevelt)

4.2.13 Let others lead small lives, but not you.

Let others argue over small things, but not you.

Let others cry over small hurts, but not you.

Let others leave their future in someone else's hand, but not you" (Jim Rohn)

The pen that writes your life story must be held in your own hand Irene C. kassorla)

4.2.14 The dreadfulness of an oracle comes from its shrine (Zhoa African proverb) This means that the greatness of a human being stems from his or her up bringing

4.2.15 Our background and circumstances may have influenced who we are, but we are responsible for who we become (Barbara Geraci)

4.2.16 Life is not about finding yourself. Life is about creating yourself (George Bernard)

4.2.17 The mediocre teacher tells. The good teacher explains. The superior teacher demonstrates. The great teacher inspires (William Arthur Ward)

4.2.18 Children need models rather than critics (Joseph Joubert)

1.2.19 A good listener is not only popular everywhere, but after a while he knows something (Wilson Mizner)

4.2.20 If you want to go quickly, go alone,

If you want to go far, go together (African proverb)

4.2.21 What most people need to learn in life is how to love people and use things instead of using people and loving things.

4.2.22 No act of kindness, however small, is ever wasted (Aesop)

4.2.23 Create a set of great personal values and surround yourself with the right people that can form your support system. Have an optimistic spirit and develop a strong purpose that you completely believe in and everything you can imagine is possible for you (Andrew Horton)

4.2.24 Success is not the key to happiness. Happiness is the key to success. If you love what you are doing, you will be successful (Herman Cain)

4.2.25 We make a living by what we get. We make a life by what we give" (Winston Churchill)

4.2.26 You can't help someone get up a hill without getting closer to the top yourself (H. Norman Schwarzkopf)

4.2.27 Open your arms to change but don't let go of your values (Dalai Lama)

4.2.28 The world is a dangerous place to live not because of the people who are evil, but because of the people who don't do anything about it (Albert Einstein)

4.2.29 It is easy to dodge our responsibilities, but we cannot dodge the consequences of dodging our responsibilities (Sir Josiah stamp)

4.2.30 You never change things by fighting the existing reality. To change something, build a new model that makes the existing model obsolete (R Buckminster Fuller).

4.2.31 If you are seeking revenge, start by digging two graves (Ancient Chinese proverb)

4.2.32 Life 's not about waiting for the storms to pass --- it's about learning to dance in the rain (B. J. Gallagher)

4.2.33 Great masters merit emulation, not Worship (Alan Cohen).

4.2.34 It's not differences that divide us. It's our judgments about each other that do (Margaret Wheatley)

4.2.35 It is understanding that gives us an ability to have peace. When we understand the other fellow's view point, and he understands ours, then we can sit down and work out our differences (Harry S. Truman)

4.2.36 Management is doing things right; leadership is doing the right things (Peter F. Druker)

4.2.37 If your actions inspire others to do more, to learn more, to dream more or to become more, you are a leader (John Quincy Adams)

4.2.38 A candle loses nothing by lighting another candle (BBC proverb)

4.2.39 An army of sheep led by a lion will always defeat an army of lions headed by a sheep (BBC proverb)

4.2.40 A cow that enjoys the company of a donkey soon learns how to kick its master (BBC proverb)

4.2.41 If you quarrel with a monkey don't accept a baboon to be your judge (BBC proverb)

4.2.42 A swamp of bees cannot storm a flower that does not smell nectar (BBC proverb)

4.2.43 Sugar cane is not eaten because it is tall and fat but because it is sweet (BBC proverb)

4.2.44 The truth passes through fire without a burn (BBC proverb)

4.2.45 A hand that always gives always gathers (BBC proverb)

4.2.46 Only a dull cock thinks that if it does not crow, the day will not break. (BBC proverb)

4.2.47 A tree that has defeated an axe cannot be cut by a knife (BBC proverb)

4.2.48 He who considers where the bee is dying will never get the sweetness of its honey (BBC proverb)

4.2.49 A fish start rottening from the head (BBC proverb)

4.2.50 A tree once struck by lightening is not scared by the darkening clouds (BBC proverb)

4.3   Conclusion

This chapter has highlighted some words which are rich in meaning. Some of these words are familiar to some students and others are not. Majority of our students at all levels have derailed because they lacked some basic orientations in their lives. As you can read above, outstanding human beings coin these words of wisdom. The speakers range from intellectuals, technicians, scientists to presidents of countries. A keen student will agree with us that success does not only go to intelligent students but also to those who are honest and even stupid. It suffices for students to be focused and move closer to wise people and they will be enlightened on the wisdoms of this world in many domains. One time reading over these words of wisdom does not suffice, so students and others are advised to read this chapter as many times as possible until the find success

References

Ashley international (2016) Identifying Your Core Values: FREE ONLINE WORKSOP to master the job hunt at land more job offers.com

BBC (2000), Focus on Africa

Circle of life wellness coaching () Your Personal Core Values: Circle of life, 5276

Hollister Ave Ste 257, Santa Barbara, ca 93111805-617-3390

http://www.circleoflefe.net

Culture action Europe (2018) The value and values of culture: European cultural foundation.

Farah, M.A et al (ED.) (1997) World History, National Geography Society; Glencoe; McGraw-Hill. New York. New York Columbus, Ohio Mission Hill, California Peoria, Illinois

Gusenmeyen, D. () Mission, Vision, Values and Goals, Sr. Exclusion Associate,

PRO- DAIRY.

Fishman, T. (1999) The Fundamental Values of Academic Integrity:

Clemson University.

Frey, R. (1994) *A Definition of "Cultural Values" be they American Indian or Euro-American*; from Rodney Frey. Eye Juggling: Seeing the World Through a Looking Glass and a Glass Pane (A Workbook for Clarifying and Interpreting Values). University Press of America: Lanham, New York, London. 1994pp 19-24

Frondizi, R. Fantauzz; C. Colasanti, N. Fiovani G. (2019). *The evaluation of Universities third*

mission and intellectual capital: Theorical analysis and application to Italy, in sustainability

2019, 3455; doi: 10.3390/su 11123455.www.mdip.com/journal/sustainability

Gündüz, M. (2016) *Classifying Values by Categories*:in journal of education and

training studies vol. 4, n°10, October 2016 issn 2324-805X e-issn 2324-8068

published by Redfaune publishing URL: http://jets.refaune.com

Gusenmeyen, D. () Mission, Vision, Values and Goals, Sr. Exclusion Associate,

PRO- DAIRY.

Highland Consulting Group, Inc (2014) Personal Values: leading with impact. your

ripple effect copyright(C)2014Highland consulting group Inc.ww.Asl.Rowi.com

Hornby, A. S. ed. (2006), Oxford Advanced Learners Dictionary,7th edition

Jennifer Kennymore, MPH, CHES Health education wellness services jeken@ in wmissouri.edu 660.562.1348.

Kivunja, C. and Kuyini A. B. (2017), *Understanding and applying Research Paradigms in Educational contexts,* in International Journal of Higher Education vol. 6, n°5; 2017.

kostinai, E. krebova, L. Tereshava, R. Tsepkova A. Vezirov T. (2015), *Universal*

Human Values: Cross Cultural Comparative Analysis in Worldwide Trend in the Development of Education and Academic Research, 15-18 June 2015 at www.sciencedirect.com

kostinai, E. krebova, L. Tereshava, R. Tsepkova A. Vezirov T. (2015), *Universal Human Values: Cross Cultural Comparative Analysis* in Worldwide Trend in the Development of Education and Academic Research, 15-18 June 2015 at

www.sciencedirect.com

Krishnamurti (), Education and the Significance of Life

Kum. J. N (2016). A Discourse Analysis of Students' Essays in Cameroon English:

PhD Thesis University of Yaounde 1

Kum. J. N. (2014). A Discourse of Adaptation: Great Experiences; USA. Amazon

Leading with Impact: Your Ripple Effect (2014). Personal Values Copyright2014 Highland Consulting Group, Inc. AskRoxi www AskRoxi.com

Lee, H. (2014) Essentials of Behavioural Science Research. California state

university, Distributed by www.lulu.com   Morrisville, NC 27560.

Lincoln – Douglas Debabe () Tynes of Values.

Mashlah, S. (2015), *The Role of People's Personal Values in the Workplace*, in International Journal of Management and Applied science. ISSN: 2394-7926, volume I, Issue-9, oct., 2015.

Matsumoto D. (2007) culture context, and behaviour in journal of personality 75: b,

December 2007c) 2007 copyright the authors journal complication C) 2007,

Blackwell publishing Inc. Doi: 10 IIII/J. 1467-6494-2007. 00476.x

McKay, J. P., Hill, B.D., & Buckler, J., (eds). (1983) *A History of Western Society*. University

of Illinois, Urbana Houghton Mifflin Company Boston Dallas Geneva, Illinois Lawrenceville

New Jersey Palo Alto

Mihelic, K.K. et als (2010) Ethical Leadership. In *International Journal of*

Management and Information Systems. Fourth Quarter 2010. Volume 14, Number 5

Naagavazan R. S. (2006) *A Textbook on Professional Ethnic and Human Values.*

New age international publishers.

Nazam, F and Husain, A. (2016) Exploring Spiritual Values Among School

Children: in International *Journal of School and Cognitive Psychology* Doi: 10.4172/2 469-9837. /000175.

NEA () Preparing 21st Century Students for a Glossal Society; National Education

Association.

NEASC (2016) Guide to Developing and Implementing CORE Values, Beliefs,

and Learning Expectation .3Burlington Woods Drive, Suite 100, Burlington, ma 01803-4514USA (781)425-7700\Fax (718) 4251001\cpss.neasc.org\Neasc.org\cps

OECD (2015), Frascati Manual 2015; Guidelines for collecting and reporting Data

on research and experimental development, the measurement of scientific,

technological and innovation activities, OECD publishing, Paris DOI:

http://dx.doi.org/10.1787/9789264239012-en

Rokeach M. (1973), The Nature of Human Values

Sari, N (2013) The Importance of Teaching Moral Values to the Students English Education Study Program of Indonesia University of Education.

Shepherd, p. (2016) Words of Wisdom https://trans4mind.com

Sun S. (2011), *Cultural Values and their Challenges for Enterprises*

in www.ijbc.webs.com International Journal of Business and Commerce vol., n°1; Sep. 2011 (10-17).

Taproot: http://www.rapport.com/archive/37771) migself

The management 3.o "B.G VALUES LIST management 30. Com

Tomar, B. (2014), *Axiology in Teacher Education: implementation and challenges,* In /OSR journal of research & method in education (IOSR-JRME) e-ISSN:2320-7388, P-ISSN: 2320-F37X: volume 4, issue 2 ver.III (Mars-April – 2014) pp.51-54www.IOSrjournal.org.

Uudom, C. (2008), Portuguese Cultural Standards from the Swedish Perspective:

A dissertation submitted as partial requirement for the conferral of Master in

international management un published.

Wibowo, T.S. et al. (2020). Effect of Hard Skills, Soft Skills, Organizational Learning and

Innovation Capability on Islamic University Lecturers' Performance, in *Sys Rev Pharm (7):*

556-569.

About the Author

Julius Nang Kum

Julius Nang Kum was born on the 5th November,1975 in Zhoa, the Headquarters of Fungom subdivision. He attended Catholic school Mekaf where he obtained his Religious and First School Leaving certificates respectively. He pursued his studies in GHS Wum, and graduated with the Ordinary and Advanced Level certificates. Kum was admitted into the University of Yaounde 1 in the Department of Linguistics where he obtained his Bachelor degree, Master's degree, his DEA and his PhD with distinctions. At the moment, he lectures at the Department of English Modern Letters in the Institution of Higher Teacher Training College of the University of Yaounde 1, Cameroon.

www.ingramcontent.com/pod-product-compliance
Lightning Source LLC
LaVergne TN
LVHW041546070526
838199LV00046B/1848